For Roger the Shrubber

IMPRINT
A part of Macmillan Publishing Group, LLC

ABOUT THIS BOOK
Artist's medium is digital, Photoshop, and Wacom Cintiq. The text was set in Caecilia LT,
and the display type is hand-drawn. The book was edited by Erin Stein
and designed by Natalie C. Sousa. The production was supervised by John Nora,
and the production editor was Hayley Jozwiak.

Library of Congress Cataloging-in-Publication Data is available.
ISBN 978-1-250-12394-7 (hardcover)

Our books may be purchased in bulk for promotional, educational,
or business use. Please contact your local bookseller or the
Macmillan Corporate and Premium Sales Department at (800) 221-7945 ext. 5442
or by e-mail at MacmillanSpecialMarkets@macmillan.com.

Imprint logo designed by Amanda Spielman

First Edition—2017

1 3 5 7 9 10 8 6 4 2

mackids.com

Don't steal this book without permission from the gnome who owns it or you'll get
the cold shoulder from everygnome. And you can take that to the snowbank.

GAME of GNOMES

Kirsten Mayer

illustrated by Laura K. Horton

{Imprint}
MAKE YOUR MARK

NEW YORK

Meet Ginger the Gnome.

Everygnome in the garden knows her by her curly red hair.

"It's so red!"

"It's so curly!"

"There's Ginger!"
"Who?"

"The redhead."
"Oh, right, the redhead!"

Ginger would rather just be called Ginger.

"Do you want a new haircut?"
asks her friend Al.

"No, I like my hair," Ginger says.
"I just want to be known for something else.
I can run fast and jump high
and catch the wind!"

"Well, winter is coming," says Gnorm.

"He means the Winter Gnome Games," says Al with a nod.
"Why don't you compete? I bet you'll win!"

"I'll do it!" says Ginger.
"I can rock this!"

The Parade of Gnomes is the very next day.

Everygnome in the garden is excited
for the Winter Gnome Games.

Even the squirrels wake up for it!

The first sport Ginger tries is sledding.

"It will be way more fun if I shred this hill standing up!" She hops on the pinecone shingle sled and pushes off.

She surfs down the hill and finishes faster than all the other gnomes!

The crowd cheers and whistles. "Go, Red!"

Ginger frowns. "That's not my name."

"That was amazing," cheers Al.

"Everygnome is going to start snowboarding now," says Gnorm.

From the judges' table, there is whispering.
Englebert, the Grandmaster of the Gnome Games, frowns over his glasses.

"Disqualified!" he grumbles.
"You are supposed to *sit* on
a sled, not stand on it!"

Gnomes glide out onto the ice rink and pirouette for the figure skating competition.

Ginger feels a need for speed—she races around the track and throws in a spin at the end. "Ta-da!"

"Disqualified!" yells Englebert. "You didn't hit the snow bunny pose.
You're on thin ice!"

"Wow, Ginger. You were super fast. You're the best skater I've ever seen!" says Al.

"Thanks, but I still didn't win."

Bartleby shouts,
"Hey, Curly, better luck next time!"

Ginger gives him the
cold shoulder.

"I have to win my next event!" she says. "I'm on a curling team."

"Why curling?" asks Gnorm.

"The ice hockey teams were full!"

Ginger steps out onto the ice with Earl, Cliff, and Eunice.
When she sees Englebert take off his cap to scratch his head,
Ginger can't resist showing off her perfect aim.

She turns the broom over and whacks the curling stone so that it sails through
the air and right into the whiskered gnome's red cap. "GOAL!" she shouts.

Englebert frowns.

DISQUALIFIED

"Impressive aim,
but this isn't hockey."

Ginger sighs. She sits down to lace her skates back up.
Behind her, Al trims the squirrel's bushy tail for the closing ceremony.

But when a finch flies by, it scares the squirrel—
who leaps away, with Al along for the ride!

Ginger springs into action.
She grabs a pinecone sled and
races down the hill.

Then she leaps onto the ice of a frozen puddle
and skates across so fast she's a blur.

"I'm coming, Al!"

She grabs a twig, swings at a small frozen mushroom,
and whizzes the cap into the bushes ahead of the runaway squirrel.

All the snow shakes loose, falls into a heap,
and stops the squirrel in its tracks.

Al lands safely in the snowbank with a *plop*.

"Thanks, Ginger! You saved me! That was the best gnomework I've ever seen," says Al.

"You're welcome. I do my best for my friends."

Everygnome saw Ginger's daring rescue. They carry Ginger and Al on their shoulders, cheering as they go.

"Ginger, the hero!"

"Ginger has perfect aim!"

"Ginger is the fastest gnome ever!"

Back at the Games, Englebert walks over to Ginger
and hangs a medal around her neck.

"Ginger, you are getting a special prize. For excellent athletic skill
used in a search and rescue mission, you are the winner of
the daisy medal for Best All-Around Gnomework!"

Everygnome cheers as loudly as they can.
Ginger the gnome smiles. She is known for
something other than her red hair!

After much celebrating, Ginger skis through the garden to go home.

Inside, her brothers and sisters pile on top of her. "We want to be in the Gnome Games, too!" they cry.

"Have you ever heard of a rodeo?"